MR 2 '01

Stay Away from
SIMON!

Also by Carol Carrick
Illustrated by Donald Carrick

What a Wimp!
Some Friend!

Stay Away from SIMON!

by CAROL CARRICK
Pictures by DONALD CARRICK

Clarion Books

TICKNOR & FIELDS: A HOUGHTON MIFFLIN COMPANY
New York

Clarion Books
a Houghton Mifflin Company imprint
215 Park Avenue South, New York, NY 10003
Text © 1985 by Carol Carrick
Illustrations © 1985 by Donald Carrick

Printed in the U.S.A.

Library of Congress Cataloging in Publication Data

Carrick, Carol.
Stay away from Simon!
Summary: Lucy and her younger brother examine their
feelings about a mentally handicapped boy they both fear
when he follows them home one snowy day.
1. Children's stories, American. [1. Mentally handicapped—Fiction]
I. Carrick, Donald, ill. II. Title.
PZ7.C2344St   1985   [Fic]   84-14289
ISBN 0-89919-343-9   PA ISBN 0-89919-849-X

QUM 20 19 18 17 16 15 14 13 12

To Pam Goff

Contents

Stay Away from
SIMON!

I.

In the Schoolyard

It was snowing again. Lucy and her little brother, Josiah, had just reached school when they saw Simon standing in the road. The children in the schoolyard were happily screeching, throwing handfuls of snow on one another. But there was something about the way that Simon stood watching them that chilled Lucy. She clutched the hood of her cloak tightly at her throat as she and Josiah passed him.

Her brother ran off to help build a snow fort, but Lucy hurried to the oak tree at the edge of the schoolyard. The branches of the old tree grew almost to the ground. In warmer weather, Lucy and her friend, Desire, sat on one of them and talked through recess. Now, out of habit, they still met there. Desire's family lived above the general store nearby, and she always got to school first.

"The miller's boy is here!" Lucy whispered. "He's standing over there. Don't look!"

But Desire turned to look anyway. "Simon? What is *he* doing here?"

Simon worked at the grist mill. When the mill was not busy, he drove the oxen on the miller's farm. Last fall when Lucy's father brought corn to be ground, Simon had unloaded the heavy sacks from their wagon. The boy's shoulders were broad as a man's, and a few dark hairs bristled on his chin. But Lucy remembered how his face had flushed with childlike pleasure at the bright penny Father had given him.

Lucy had never seen Simon at school before. She had heard that he used to come when the pond froze and the mill wheel was locked in ice. Like many of the older boys on the farms in West Tisbury, the miller's boy could only be spared from work in the dead of winter.

But Simon was different. His mind was too slow

for schooling. When he could not learn to read or even count, he struck out at the boys who called him "Simple Simon." Once he caught Everett Allen in the face with his elbow. When Simon saw the red blood gush from the boy's nose, he ran off to the woods. He hid from everyone, even the miller, until the cold drove him home. After that he would not go back to school, ever. Some said it didn't matter—he was no more than an animal, like the big, dumb oxen he cared for.

Simon never hung about with boys his own age, but he liked little children. He was often seen watching the small boys who fished in the mill pond. Sometimes he offered them a top or a whistle he had made. But many of the parents thought this was not natural. "Stay away from Simon," they warned.

"Remember the Tilton boy?" Desire said to Lucy as they huddled on the branch of the oak tree. "They used *our wagon* to take him home."

Lucy shivered. The men had found his body under the ice. It was said that Simon had been at the pond when Ben Tilton drowned. From then on, even the children shied away from him and would not take his gifts.

Over near the fort there was shouting. A snowball fight had started. Most of the children ran to join in. Desire jumped up from the branch and Lucy started to follow her.

"Hey!" Lucy yelped as a shower of snow caught her by surprise. Laughing, she pushed off her hood and shook it. She turned to see which of her friends had dumped the snow.

Lucy gave a little gasp and her smile disappeared. It was Simon. He must have sneaked up while she and Desire were talking. Now he stood grinning, crouched like a playful dog waiting to be chased.

"Don't do that!" Lucy said sharply. But before she could put her hood back on, Simon scooped up more snow and threw it at her.

"Stop! Stop it!" she demanded.

Desire was too startled to say anything.

Simon grew more excited, whipping up whole armloads of snow and showering himself and Lucy with the powdery stuff. She backed away from him, shielding her face with her arms. Lucy looked around for help, but all the older boys were defending their snow fort.

"I'll get Master Hume," Desire said, running

toward the schoolhouse.

Now Simon was laughing, screwing up his face horribly and waving his clenched fists. Lucy turned away and brushed the snow from her hair and cloak. Simon came closer until he could reach out and touch her hair.

"Don't touch me! Go away . . ." Lucy commanded.

"SNOW," he said, brushing her long curls. She was surprised at his deep voice.

Nearby, children had stopped to watch them. Some gave each other timid looks. A few were laughing; others were afraid to move. Staring at the ground, they hoped that Simon would not pick on them next.

Before Desire got to him, the schoolmaster appeared in the doorway ringing his bell. A last snowball was thrown. The children crowded around the door, chattering noisily and shoving to be first inside to warm themselves. In this stir, Simon disappeared.

Lucy tried to blend into the crowd, tears of outrage and embarrassment stinging her eyes. But Desire burrowed in beside her and tugged at her clothes.

"Tell him!" Desire urged, pushing her toward the schoolmaster.

"Shh!" Lucy shook her head impatiently. She didn't want to attract any more attention to what had happened.

Inside, Lucy took as long as she could to remove her mittens and cloak. There were not enough pegs, and as the smallest children jumped to hang their clothes, other scarves and coats slid to the ground and were trampled. Lucy hung up some of them to calm herself before joining the others.

II.

Out Early

To get order, the schoolmaster rapped loudly on his desk. The children around the stove quickly took their places. Lucy, who was eleven, sat with the big girls at a long desk nailed to the back wall.

After Lucy practiced her letters over and over on a slate, Master Hume gave her a sentence to write in her copybook. Lucy's mother had helped her make the book at home. She had folded sheets of paper that parcels came wrapped in, and sewed them together like a real book. The cover was made from heavier paper that she decorated with birds and flowers. Lucy bit her lip as she formed the letters:

With All Thy Soul Love God Above
And As Thyself Thy Neighbor Love

Even when she was careful, her pen made awful blots.

Warmth from the stove didn't reach her part of the room. Lucy tried to warm her stiff fingers under her apron. Out of the corner of her eye, she thought she caught a movement at the window. It was snowing harder now. The wind was blowing flakes through chinks in the wall where she sat.

After the lunch recess, Lucy stole a look at her brother, Josiah. He was sitting on a bench up front, with the rest of the beginners. His face was still red from playing outside, and being so close to the fire was making him sleepy. His eyes closed and his head nodded as the master's voice droned on.

Lucy didn't think Hume was fond of children or of teaching. Father said it was probably the only way he could earn a living. The year Lucy started school, George Look, the blacksmith's

son, and some other troublemakers had locked out the former schoolmaster during noon recess. The young teacher had ripped a board from the fence, climbed up on the roof, and smoked out the boys by covering up the chimney.

Lucy thought the teacher had been most clever, but the school board voted to find someone with more experience. That was why they picked Master Hume. He believed in showing rough lads from the start who was boss.

"JOSIAH BLISS!" Lucy was surprised to hear her brother's name called. "Stand up, please." Hume's voice hissed a warning.

Josiah seemed startled when he jumped to his feet. Obviously he had not been listening.

"You will be kind enough to recite the lesson," said the master.

Josiah peeked at the blackboard, but it was bare of clues. Then he looked to the other little boys for help, but they dared not turn their heads.

"I—I don't know," Josiah stuttered.

"*That* is because you are not paying attention."

Lucy chewed her lip. Poor Josey! He was so small to be starting school. But he was bright and

he had begged every day to go. The Bliss family lived a long way from the village of West Tisbury. It was a cold, dark walk to school on winter mornings. Josiah was always half-asleep, but Lucy told him if he was going to come, he would have to keep up.

Hume took a stool from the chimney corner. "Sit here for the rest of the afternoon," he said to Josiah. "It will help you to stay awake."

Josiah looked at the stool in puzzlement. Someone giggled. It had only one leg. Josiah balanced on it as well as he could.

The rest of his classmates stood, lining up their toes on a crack in the floor. Together, they started to recite their alphabet lesson. "A. In Adam's fall, we sinned All. A . . ."

Josiah's face burned with shame.

As the afternoon slowly passed, snowflakes stuck to the windows and the room got darker and darker. At last the schoolmaster cleared his throat and announced, "Since the storm is growing worse, we shall all go home after the spelling lesson."

There were shouts of joy. Josiah jumped up

27

from the stool. School was out early! West Tisbury was on the island of Martha's Vineyard in Nantucket Sound. Unlike the rest of New England, it rarely snowed there. But if the snow really piled up, it could take days for the farmers to open the roads again.

Desire walked arm in arm with Lucy as far as her father's general store. "Tell me," she said eagerly. "What did Simon do?" It made Lucy feel important, so she told Desire how he had touched her hair. "But if you tell anyone else, I'll just die!" she said. Lucy could imagine the teasing at school. "LUCY HAS A SWEETHEART!"

Josiah grew tired of throwing snowballs on the porch roof while the girls whispered together. He squinted up at the bulletin board wishing he could spell out the notices. "How long are we going to be here?" he grumbled. By this time the other children were already in their houses on Music Street or had disappeared around Brandy Brow.

"Go on ahead," Lucy said over her shoulder. "Am *I* keeping you here?" But as soon as Josiah was out of sight she hastily said good-bye to Desire and hurried after him. Mother would have a fit if Josiah told her he had walked home by himself.

III.

A Short Cut

Lucy tried to put Josiah in a holiday mood on the way home. She started a counting song to make the long walk more fun.

"One, two, buckle my shoe . . ."

Josiah enjoyed repeating the lines. "One, two, buckle my shoe . . ." At the end of the song they started over.

"Three, four, shut the door," Lucy was singing when a deep voice echoed.

"Three, four . . . DOOR!"

Lucy felt a twist of fear. She stopped and turned. It was Simon. Was he following them? The mill was nearby. Maybe he was going home.

Simon stopped a few paces away. Lucy did not feel relieved by the sly smile he gave her. To her, it had the same sweetness as the one the wolf must have given Red Riding Hood.

Simon began rocking from side to side. His reddened hands swung awkwardly from their bent wrists.

Lucy started Josiah walking again. "Pay him no mind," she said to her brother, hoping she sounded brave.

"Three, four . . . three, four . . ." Simon called after them in a singsong. Was he making fun of her?

"Pretend you don't hear him," she whispered.

"Three, four . . ." Simon started again.

Lucy whirled around and faced him. "You stop following us, Simon," she said angrily, "or I'll tell my father on you!"

"HAW, HAW, HAW!" The boy laughed loudly, but the laugh sounded forced.

"Three, four . . . Three, four . . ." he repeated, bobbing his head. He seemed to be searching his mind for something.

"DOOR!" he remembered and laughed again.

Simon began to excite himself as he had that morning. He flapped his hands and chanted,

"THREE, FOUR . . . DOOR! ONE, TWO!"

Lucy shuddered. With her arm protectively around Josiah, she backed away.

Suddenly Simon's mood changed. He frowned and shook his head violently. Lucy could not tell what he was thinking, but the snow was piling up quickly and they had a long way to go. "Come on, Josey," she said.

Whenever Josiah tried to look back, Lucy jerked his arm. "Keep walking!"

After they passed the empty Mayhew place, the road became a wagon track that wound through fields and woods for several miles. Lucy stopped a moment and took a deep breath. She had to make a decision. She didn't want to be

caught with Simon on this lonely stretch. If she had to call for help, no one would hear her. But what other choice did she have?

Lucy looked quickly over her shoulder. Simon had dropped behind. He would not be able to see them after they passed the place where the road curved sharply. With the wind whipping snow in his face, he might not notice that their tracks had left the road.

"Quick!" Lucy urged Josiah, giving him a shove when they turned the corner. "Cut through the woods."

Lucy pushed between fir trees that grew thickly here. Snow slid off the branches and showered on their heads. As soon as the trees hid them, Lucy put her fingers over Josiah's lips. She held him still and listened. She could hear nothing but the pounding of her heart and the hiss of the falling snow.

They waited, giving Simon enough time to pass. Then Lucy whispered, "Follow me." They could cut through the woods and come out on the road to their farm.

Lucy was careful to hold back the branches so they would not whip into Josiah's face. At first they tried not to make sounds that would give them away. But they could not avoid snapping the dead branches underfoot. Then they just made a run for it, stumbling in holes and tripping. Lucy's long skirts got in the way, and her hair became caught when they crawled through the thickets.

"Can't we stop a minute?" Josiah begged.

"We're almost to our road," said Lucy. But now she was struck by doubt. Why was it taking so long? She stopped to get her bearings. If they were going the right way, the sun would be over their shoulder. She squinted up through the flakes. All she could see was gray sky and falling snow. Lucy looked around desperately. Was she leading them in circles?

Lucy found them a sheltered spot under the roots of a fallen tree. They sat on the ground together and shared the leftover corn bread and dried apples that mother had given them for lunch. Now that they were not walking, it was cold.

While they rested, Lucy decided what to do. If we try to keep going in one direction, she reasoned, we have to come out *somewhere*. They started walking again. It was hard to keep straight as the crow flies, because of the heavy underbrush. But sure enough, after a while, it looked clearer ahead.

"Josey, there's the road!" Lucy said, with great relief. "It won't be long now till we're home."

At the edge of the woods, Lucy stopped in confusion. It was not the road at all. It was someone's field. But whose? Dear God, she thought, what have I done? We're lost.

Lucy chose a new direction so their backs would be to the wind, and she tried to sound cheery. "We'll come to the road very soon," she said. When Josiah looked doubtful she added, "And maybe we'll stop at the first house we see to get warm."

What house? They had not seen a building for almost an hour.

IV.

Lost in the Snow

As the day got late, Lucy and Josiah plowed on through more of the strange countryside.

Now that they were out of the woods, Lucy was sure they would see a familiar landmark. But under the cover of snow, the roads and even some of the stone walls had disappeared. Like sand dunes shifted by the wind, the snow had shaped a new landscape. Not a soul, not another living creature did they see. It was as if the blowing snow had scoured everything away.

"Lucy, I'm so tired," whined Josiah. Snow reached above his knees now, even higher where it had drifted. His heavy clothing was wet through.

"We *have* to keep going, Josey," she pleaded.

"We mustn't stop here."

"But I can't walk any more, Lucy. I can't!" The little boy started to sob.

"Oh Josey!" Lucy took him in her arms and rocked him against her. His cap was icy next to her chapped face. Josiah trusted her. How could she tell him that now they were really lost?

She thought with growing panic about old Tim Sleeper. He had been one of the harmless, good-for-nothings who gathered every day on the post-office porch. Full of whiskey, he had lost his way one night last January and froze to death.

"Don't cry, Josey. Please don't," Lucy said, but now she was crying herself. It was too late. They would never find their way home.

Without warning and without a sound, the miller's boy suddenly appeared beside them. He must have been tracking them. Lucy screamed. In that snowy wilderness her scream sounded thin, like a rabbit struck by a hawk.

Simon pulled Josiah away from her. Holding the little boy's wrist, he sank to his knees.

"Don't hurt him!" Lucy pleaded. "He's so little."

"Under!" growled Simon, holding up the back of his woolen smock. It was twice too big for him, probably a castoff of the miller's.

Josiah gave his sister a frightened look. What was Simon going to do?

Lucy nodded. "It's all right," she said. To encourage Josiah she tried to smile. "Do what he says. You'll get warm." But she was sick with fear. How could they escape from Simon now?

Josiah crawled under the smock. Simon pulled his own arms out of the sleeves and hooked them under Josiah's legs. Then he rose to his feet, carrying the little boy piggyback.

"Hold on!" Simon shouted and began walking. Did he mean her? Lucy was not sure.

"Lucy?" Josiah cried out. "Don't leave me!"

"I'm here, Josey!" she called, running to catch up. She grabbed the flapping sleeve of Simon's smock so that she would not be blown away.

Then Lucy had an idea. To soothe Josiah, she began to sing the counting rhyme again. "Three, four, shut the door. Five, six, pick up sticks." The wind snatched her words and flung them over her shoulder.

"Five, six, pick up sticks," piped a muffled voice from the hump on Simon's back.

Over and over, Lucy drilled as they slogged on. "Seven, eight, lay them straight." It kept her going.

Lucy's toes ached so with the cold that she feared they would snap at the next step. Once she stumbled and fell. Her hand was numb, but stubbornly she clung to the empty sleeve. She must not be separated from her brother.

"One . . . two . . . buckle my . . . shoe." Lucy was so thirsty that the words were like ashes in her mouth. "Three . . . four . . ."

Simon was muttering to himself. Did she risk making him angry with her singsong? She continued the chant anyway. It was her only way to comfort Josiah. As long as he could hear her, he would know that she was still with him.

Finally Lucy grew silent except for her hoarse breathing. All her concentration was on keeping up with Simon. She stared blindly at the ground ahead of her, willing first one leg and then the other to move until they grew too heavy. At last she dropped Simon's sleeve and let herself sink down. It felt so good, giving up to the snow. She would just shut her eyes. Sleep for a while. And forget.

"UP!" shouted Simon.

Lucy paid no attention.

"GE-UP!"

Flinching from his command, Lucy protected her head with her arms as if to ward off a blow. "Please," she begged. "Leave me alone."

"Wu-cy," he said more gently, nudging her with his foot. "WU-CY!"

She looked up at him. Simon's cap was pulled so low that his eyes appeared as two dark holes. He was iced over like a monster from some nightmare tale. Lucy looked away. It was then that she saw the dark figure on horseback coming down the hill toward them. She knew the broad shoulders, the shape of his hat.

Father!

Lucy struggled to her feet and waved her arms. "Father!"

His arm raised in answer.

"Josey! Josey! It's Father. He's found us!" She thumped the bulge on Simon's back.

"Put him down!" she shrieked at Simon, pulling at the hump on his back. "Put him down. My father's come."

Lucy was crying again. She beat on Simon, sobbing and trying to catch her breath. Simon released Josiah's legs and the boy slid down his back. Her brother looked red and wrinkled as he emerged from under the coarse shirt.

"I've been looking everywhere for you," Father said, leaning from his horse. "I've been up and down the road, but I couldn't find you."

"We got lo-ost," Lucy tried to explain between sobs. "We cut through the woods . . . and I couldn't find the road . . . and *he* came after us!"

"Now, now, we'll talk after we get home," Father said.

Simon lifted Josiah to the front of Father's

saddle. Lucy allowed him to give her a leg up onto the wide back of their farm horse. She put her arms around Father's waist, leaning her head against him as he clucked to the horse. Simon followed on foot.

Without Lucy's notice, the snow had gradually stopped. Now the sky was tinted the pink and gold of a shell. Suddenly she recognized the windbreak of pines planted to shelter their road. An uncomfortable lump swelled in her throat as she understood. Simon and the miller's oxen had been loaned to half the farmers in West Tisbury. He must have known where he was all along. He had been taking them home.

V.

By the Stove

Mother was graining the sheep in the barn. When she saw that Lucy and Josiah were safe, she rushed to hug them. Then she began to fuss at them, shaking the snow from their clothes and pushing back Josiah's wet hair. In one of the stalls, the cow threw back her head and bawled for attention.

"Never mind her, Mother, I'll do the milking," Father said. "You take care of *them*." He nodded at the children.

On the way out, Mother was startled when Simon stepped from the shadow of the doorway.

"Simon found us. He was bringing us home," Lucy explained. Simon ducked his face away and grinned sheepishly, rubbing the back of his neck in a self-conscious way.

"Come in. Come in." Mother shooed Simon in the direction of the house. "You need to get by the stove."

But Simon shook his head. "No. Go home."

"Not tonight, boy. Not in the dark," called Father. He was a man of few words, and when he said something, folks generally listened.

That evening the family ate silently. The children were not used to having a stranger at the table. But Father attempted to be sociable. He spoke to Simon in a hearty way that did not sound like himself.

"Well! I guess there will be plenty of work for a good team of oxen tomorrow . . . clearing the roads."

Simon continued to eat as though he had not heard.

Mother offered him more of the mutton stew. The boy refused in a voice so low she had to repeat her question. Even though Lucy was grateful to Simon, she thought he was being rude.

Simon was offered a bed by the kitchen stove, but he preferred to sleep in the barn. After Simon left, Josiah was put to bed. Then Lucy told how Simon had appeared at school that morning and followed them home.

Excused from her chores, Lucy stayed at the table watching the smoke from Father's pipe while Mother hummed at the sink. Scenes of the schoolyard and the snow-filled woods whirled inside her head. Could it all have happened this same day? It seemed part of a dream.

Mother rattled the iron rings on the wood stove. "I'm fixing some hot cider for you to take out to the boy," she said.

"Mother, must I?" Lucy shrank from the thought of facing Simon alone.

"Seems he put himself to a lot of trouble for you," said Father.

"He didn't have to follow us after school," said Lucy. As if the blame were hers! "We wouldn't have gotten lost if he hadn't scared us like that."

With a nail, Father carefully scraped the ashes from his pipe.

"Desire says that Simon is not the miller's son

at all. She says he's the child of the Devil," said Lucy.

"Desire and her notions!" Mother held the platter she was wiping against her apron. "I remember when that boy was born. His mother was so proud. Simon was their only child that lived." She shook her head sadly.

Lucy defended her feelings. "Desire's brother

has heard wicked stories about Simon. But he says he cannot tell them to her."

Father groaned. "I'm sure her brother hears all kinds of things, working at that store. Most of them are probably not fit to be repeated."

"But what about the Tilton boy," Lucy said. "He *was* drowned. And Simon was there."

Father leaned forward and covered her hand with his own. His palm was hard and dry. "It does great harm to tell stories like that, Lucy. Every year some boy wants to be the first to cross the ice on Mill Pond. It wasn't the only time Ben Tilton fell through. The fact was that Simon tried to pull him out. He was soaking wet when he ran to the store for help, but he was too worked up at the time to explain what happened."

Lucy lowered her eyes from Father's. Maybe so, she thought. But that still didn't explain why Simon had followed them on the road. And he still made her feel uncomfortable.

As soon as the cider was hot, Lucy's mother held out her own shawl. "When you come back," she said, "there will be a nice hot cup waiting for you."

VI.

Nine, Ten, Big Fat Hen

Outside the sky was clear now, open to the stars. Lucy stepped carefully into Simon's footprints, trying not to spill the steaming cup of cider.

Inside, the barn was very dark.

"Simon?" Lucy called timidly. She hoped he would not jump out at her. The horse looked over its stall and the loose sheep came and jostled her, expecting a treat. "Simon? Are you here?" Lucy's eyes darted from corner to dark corner. He was gone, she hoped.

Then she heard a murmur in the low haymow overhead. Lucy raised her candle. Simon was lying in the loose hay. His eyes were fixed on the rafters

and he was talking to himself. Could he be pray-
ing? As Lucy backed away he turned to her.

"What?" he said gruffly, sitting up and throwing a stable blanket from his shoulders.

"Mother sent you this hot cider." Her voice
was hesitant.

Simon grunted, rolling to his knees, and backed
down the ladder.

Lucy held out the mug, unconsciously moving
away from him at the same time. "Take it. . . .
It's good."

Simon had seemed so frightening to her in the
snow. Now he looked wary, but not dangerous,
a wild creature shut up with their barn animals.

"Here. It will make you warm," Lucy urged.

Simon cupped his hands around the mug. His
fingers were surprisingly long and slender. He
snuffed the spicy steam with obvious pleasure.
Without tasting the cider, he set the mug carefully on a beam and stood rubbing the back of
his neck.

With great relief, Lucy turned to go.

"No go!" he said.

In a playful gesture, Simon laid one finger on

the side of his nose and smiled. Actually, his smile *was* sweet. The boy pulled himself up straight and took a deep breath. What was he going to do now? Lucy wondered.

"One, two . . . shoe," Simon said, as if announcing it. "Three, four . . . shut door."

He thrust his face at Lucy, waiting for her reaction.

She nodded. But why was he saying this now? Then the memory came back to her of Simon on the snowy road. She remembered him repeating her words, "THREE, FOUR . . . THREE, FOUR!" and flapping his arms like a scarecrow.

"Five, six . . . sticks," Simon was saying.

He frowned and went over it again, "Five, six, sticks," trying to find his way.

"Seven . . ." Lucy began.

"Seven, eight . . . lay straight!" Simon's words came in a rush. "NINE TEN BIG FAT HEN!" He laughed loudly, his face flushed with triumph.

A smile spread on Lucy's face and a thrill crept up her limbs. It was the feeling she got when she heard a beautiful singing voice in church. So that was why Simon had followed them!

She grabbed both of his hands. How surprised they would be at the mill tomorrow when he showed them. Simon could count to ten.